The Huddle

Sean Julian

OXFORD
UNIVERSITY PRESS

No longer an albatross chick covered in fluff, Alba now had her big-bird wings.

'Time to fly,' she said, letting the wind lift her into the sky.

Alba flew fast and far.

Far away from the things
she knew.

She looked for fish in the
water below but didn't see
the wave above.

It came crashing down . . .

. . . and dumped Alba on a rocky shore.

Her wing wouldn't move.

Too sore and too tired to fly, Alba closed her eyes and slept.

She was all alone.

But when Alba woke . . .

. . . there was a penguin.

'Squawk,' said the penguin and dropped a fish by Alba's feet.

'Is it for me?' she asked.

The penguin blinked.

Alba didn't speak penguin and the penguin didn't speak albatross.

Lots more penguins came.

Sometimes with fish but always with a friendly waddle.

Alba didn't feel alone any more.

And when danger came close . . .

. . . she felt safe.

Alba loved the penguins' playful ways. She almost forgot how much she missed the sky.

One day as the sun went down and the penguins stopped to watch it disappear, Alba thought they looked worried.

Then dark storm clouds rolled in that covered the stars.

Alba fluffed up her feathers to keep warm
but she still felt the cold wind.

As she shivered, the penguins rushed to her side

and began to huddle around her.

Alba fell asleep to the sound of
penguin hearts beating softly.

Ba-dum, ba-dum, ba-dum.

She was surrounded by love,
day after day, night after night.

When Alba woke, the storm had passed.

Penguins were everywhere – hopping, jumping, rushing onto rocks.

'Brip-brip-brip-brip!' they said.

Alba didn't need to speak penguin
to know how excited they were.

The penguins stretched out their wings and waited
for the sun. It had been dark for so, so long.

Very carefully, Alba stretched her wings too.
The broken one was mended!

It was time to fly.

'Thank you,' said Alba to her friends.

And even though Alba had been dreaming of flying away,
it was still hard for her to say goodbye.

But with the penguins cheering her on,
she held out her wings and lifted into the sky.

Alba flew fast and far.
And she never forgot the penguins.

When the time came to raise her own fluffy chick,
Alba surrounded it with love as warm
and as safe and as caring . . .

. . . as the love she had felt at the heart of the
penguin huddle.

For Merryn and
magical Auntie Floh
A S

For Iris B
N E

DEAN

First published in Great Britain 2017 by Egmont UK Limited.
This edition published 2018 by Dean,
an imprint of Egmont UK Limited,
The Yellow Building, 1 Nicholas Road, London, W11 4AN
www.egmont.co.uk

Text copyright © Amy Sparkes 2017
Illustrations copyright © Nick East 2017
Amy Sparkes and Nick East have asserted their moral rights.

ISBN 978 0 6035 7563 1
70163/006 Printed in Malaysia

A CIP catalogue record for this title is available from the British Library.

Ellie's Magic Wellies

By Amy Sparkes

Illustrated by Nick East

One miserable day it rained and it poured.
Ellie Pengelly was fed up and bored.

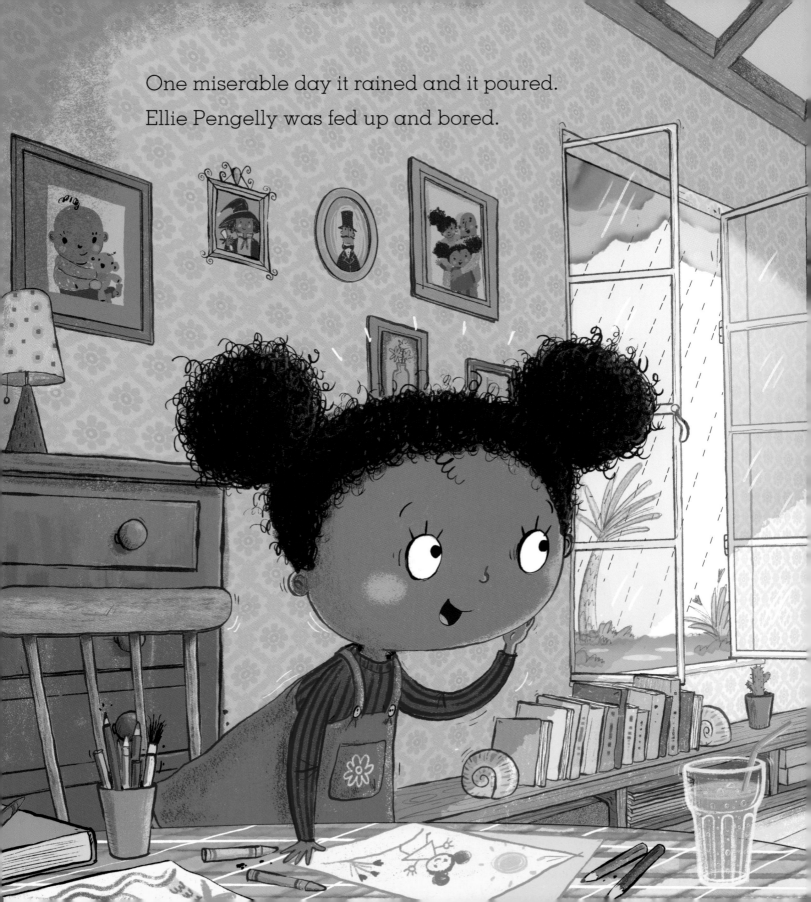

Until at the door came a *rat-a-tat-tat!*

And there stood Aunt Flo with her **marvellous** hat!

"I'm late for the dentist," said Mum. "I must go!
But you stay and play with your dear Auntie Flo."

Her aunt gave a smile,

"You won't be bored, Ellie.
I've brought you a pair of . . .

GIVE
IT
WELLIE

fantabulous wellies!"

"Oh, thanks, Auntie Flo! They're great!" Ellie cried.
"And look! It's even stopped raining outside."

"Just find some **puddles**,"
Flo called after Ellie,
"and then you'll have fun with
those wonderful wellies."

Ellie found a **big puddle** for splashing about,

but as she

j
u
m
p
e
d

in...

"My wellies are **magic!**"
cried Ellie with glee.

The creature bowed low
as he said happily,

"I'm a
Flibberty-Gibberty,
hip, hip, hooray!
I'm out of my **puddle**
and ready to **play!**

Let's wriggle! Let's giggle! Let's skip to the sky.

Play hippity-hopscotch and flap till we fly.

Let's zippedy-zoom. That's just what I like!"

The Flibberty said as he hopped on the bike.

But after a while, Ellie ran out of puff.

"I'm tired," she said.
"Haven't YOU had enough?"

"Nonsense and flip-flap," the Flibberty said. "No time for flop-flopping! Come, stand on your head!"

A thought came to Ellie,
"Let's go in and eat."

The Flibberty clapped.
"A *splendiddly* treat."

He darted inside . . .

. . . flinging open the door,
and **emptied** the fridge
out on Mum's kitchen floor!

"Let's **juggle** with jam
and **jiggle** with jelly!

Let's guzzle and gobble," he giggled to Ellie.

She looked at the floor. "We should tidy away . . ."

But Flibberty said,
"Why, there's still time to play . . .

Let's zoom through the rooms,

bounce-a-bounce on the beds.

Let's flubble with bubbles . . .

and wear **pants**
on our head!"

Then Auntie Flo called,

"That was Mum on the phone.

She rang up to say that she's
on her way home."

"Home?" squeaked Ellie. "But look at this mess!
Oh, put down that lipstick and take off that dress!

We've both turned the
house upside-down
everywhere,
but I'll be in trouble – that just isn't fair."

The Flibberty blushed.

"From my tail to my paws,

I'm most muchly SORRY

for trouble I cause."

Ellie couldn't stay cross, as she watched her friend bow,
but she needed a plan and she needed it now.

"I know," said Ellie, "now listen to me.

If we tidy together, how fast could we be?"

The Flibberty clapped, "We'll be quick as a flick.
And tidy in half of a tickety-tick!"

WHOOSH

The magical wellies made Ellie's feet zoom
and soon they had straightened up all of the rooms.

Then they ran to the garden and found Flibberty's puddle.
"I'm glad you could play!" Ellie gave him a cuddle.

"So fabbity funderful!"
her new friend said.

"But now I am ready for **snoozles** in bed."

They held hands and
jumped with a fabulous

S P L A
S
H!

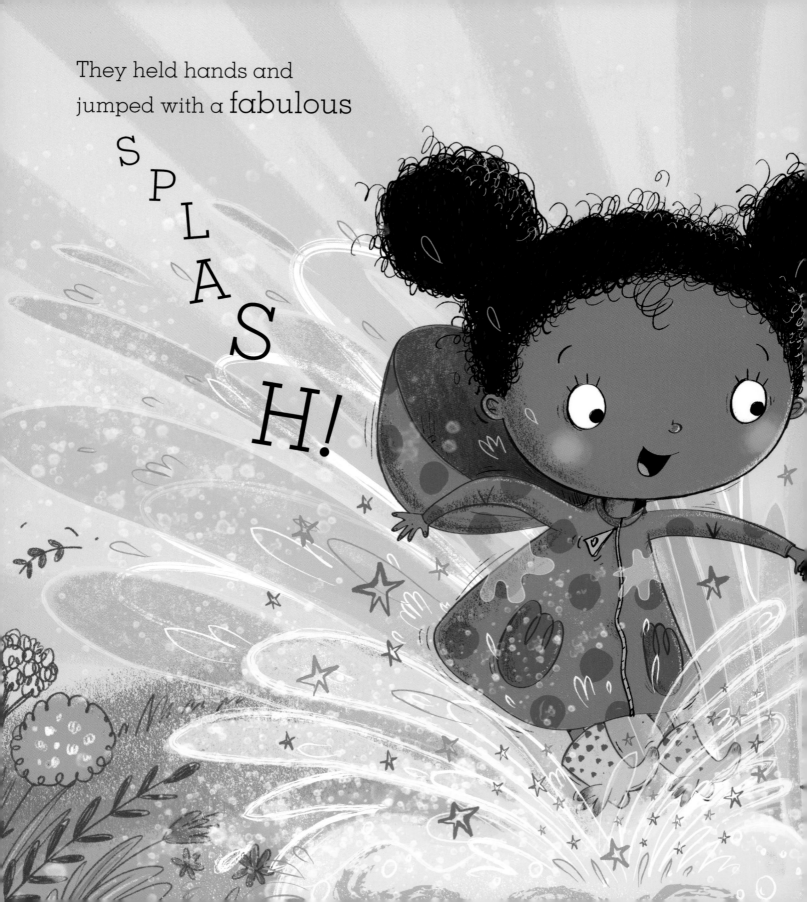

And *Flibberty* vanished as quick as a flash.

Just then Mum appeared with Aunt Flo at her side.
"Nice wellies!" said Mum. "Are you coming inside?"

"Oh no!" Ellie said.
"I would **much** rather stay
and play in our puddly
garden all day!"

"Now I'm off for another adventure," said Ellie,
"More fantabulous fun with my . . .

magical
wellies!"

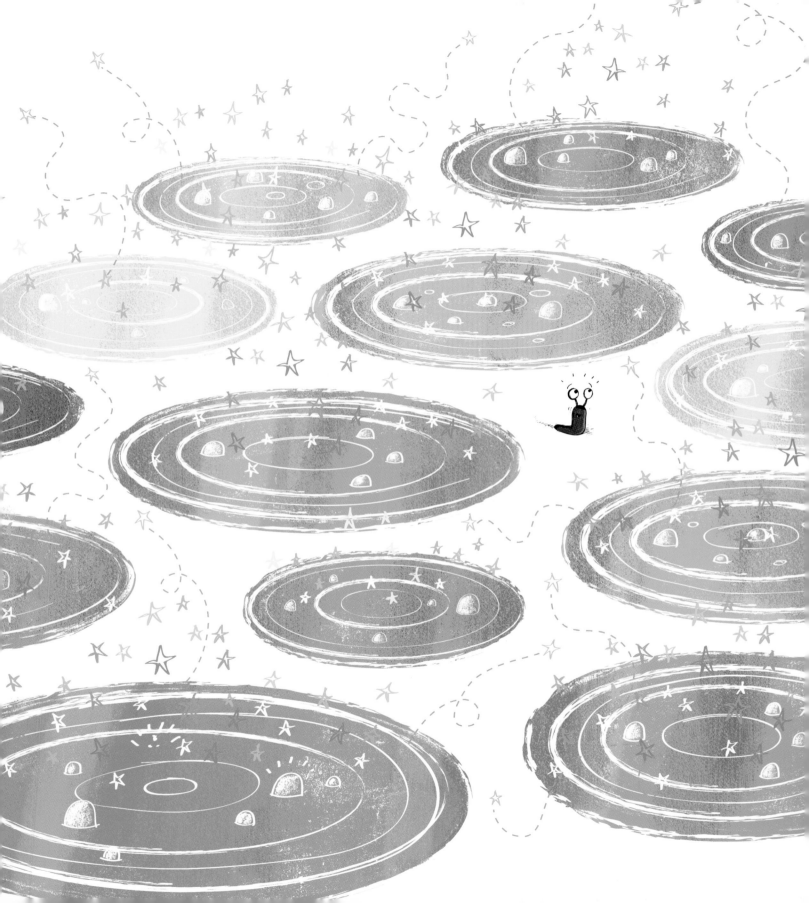